Being Oscar

Written by Kay Woodward

Illustrated by Marina Pérez Luque

Collins

Chapter 1

Oscar *loved* reading.

Once he opened a book, he could go *anywhere* and find out about *anything*. He could learn how rockets work. He could dive into a black hole. He could discover why volcanoes erupt or when dinosaurs became extinct or what the insides of a computer actually look like. A book even taught him how to juggle. (Though he wasn't very good at it.)

At home, Oscar's family knew that he sucked up facts like a vacuum cleaner sucks up carpet fluff. So they were always asking him questions.

"Oscar, what's the capital of Peru?"

"Lima."

"Oscar, why won't my computer mouse work?"

"Because it's the wrong way round."

"Oscar, if I started walking now, how long would it take me to get to the North Pole?"

"Hmm. About two years and eight months."

"Oscar, you're a genius!" they always said, which made him feel happy inside.

But at school it was a different story. There, the other children thought that Oscar was weird. They laughed at him for reading all the time, and sniggered whenever he put his hand up in class. He didn't have the chance to tell them any amazing facts because they were too busy making fun of him. They wouldn't even let him join in at football.

"No way!" said Harry. "We're not playing with *you*."

"Stick to your books, word nerd," Riley told Oscar. "Leave football to the experts."

Oscar had never played football, but he *was* a little bit of a football expert. He knew that the ball had 12 black pentagons and 20 white hexagons and that the 4-4-2 formation was very popular. But by now the boys had kicked the ball to the other end of the playground, so he couldn't tell them.

"Why won't they play with me?" Oscar asked Rahul.

"It's because you're geeky," Rahul replied helpfully. "You spend all your time with your nose in a book. When a teacher asks a question, you always know the answer. Sorry, you're just not cool."

"Oh," said Oscar. "So if I become cool, then I can play football?"

Rahul shrugged. "I suppose so," he said.

Oscar was delighted. Now that he'd found out what was wrong, he could fix the problem. He just needed someone to help him do it. And luckily, he knew the perfect person.

Chapter 2

Mo was the newest pupil at school and the coolest, too. He wore funky tortoiseshell glasses. His hair was longer on top, and he had a zigzag pattern shaved on each side.

But he didn't just *look* cool. Mo *was* cool, too. His family owned rescue cats named Ziggy and Stardust. He was vegan. One day, he was going to swim the Channel. Best of all, he was thoughtful and kind.

Harry and Riley wanted to play football with him.

Rahul wanted to find out where he got his hair done.

Everyone wanted to be around him. But Mo was so ultra-cool that no one had been brave enough to make friends with him yet.

"Mo!" said Oscar the next morning, spotting the new boy in the playground.

"Hey," replied Mo, pulling out his ear pods. "What's up?"

Oscar blurted the words straight out. "Everyone says I'm geeky," he said, "and I need to be cool instead. So I figured that since you're already cool, maybe you could help?"

"Er … sure," said Mo, not looking sure at all.

"Because I was thinking maybe a makeover might work," Oscar went on. "Would people like me more if I dyed my hair purple? Or what if I throw an enormous party and invite the whole class?"

"Definitely don't do *any* of those things," said Mo.

"*Other* people are cool," Oscar went on, pointing to a girl with long, dark hair. "Erin's cool because she can moonwalk round the whole playground without bumping into anything. Rahul can do a backflip. What will make *me* cool?"

Mo rubbed his chin. "Tell me what *you* are good at," he said.

Oscar shrugged. "I can't do anything spectacular," he replied. "I can remember facts. I can fix things. I like solving problems. You know, geeky stuff."

"Then I do have *one* idea," said Mo.

Chapter 3

The next day, Mo's backpack rattled and clunked.

"What have you got in there?" asked Harry curiously. "I didn't realise it was bring-a-toolbox-to-school day." He laughed at his own joke.

In reply, Mo turned the backpack upside down and emptied it onto the desk. A remote-controlled car fell out.

The teacher hurried over. "We only bring in toys on the last day of school, I'm afraid," Ms Swan said, picking up the car.

Mo laughed. "I don't want to *play* with this," he said. "It's stopped working and I just wondered if anyone could fix it." He shrugged helplessly. "I'm no good at that sort of thing."

"Well?" said Ms Swan, her gaze sweeping round the classroom. "Can anyone help?"

There was an awkward silence.

"Don't look at me," said Harry. "*I'm* not a geek.
I'm too busy being a champion striker to fix things.
Did you know that I can keep a football in the air for
THREE MINUTES AND 22 – ?"

"That's wonderful, Harry," said the teacher, cutting
him short. "Anyone else?"

"Can't you just buy a new one?" suggested Riley.

Ms Swan stared at Riley as if he'd just suggested
that everyone dress up as clowns and throw trifles
at each other. She spent a few minutes reminding
her class why it was so important to reduce, reuse
and recycle.

Shyly, Oscar put his hand up. "Maybe I could help?" he said.

Oscar often took things apart to see how they worked. Then he put them back together again to see if they still worked. (Usually, they did.) So it only took him a few seconds to figure out what was wrong with the car and even less time to fix it.

Shyly, he handed everything back to Mo. "The remote control's switch was on the wrong channel," he said quietly. "So I just changed it to the right one. It was easy, really."

"Pfft," said Harry. "Trust a geek to work it out."

But Mo was grinning. "Amazing," he said.

Chapter 4

"OSCAR!" Mo roared across the playground
the next morning. "CAN YOU FIX MY RUBIK'S CUBE?"

Oscar looked up from his book nervously.
Everyone was staring at him. Even the football game
had stopped. "I think so – ?" he called back.

"AWESOME!" bellowed Mo. He strolled over
to Oscar. "Because I think it must be broken.
All the colours are mixed up, and it doesn't matter
how much I twist it, I can't un-mix them."

"Hmm," said Oscar, turning the cube over and over.

Oscar had once learnt how to solve a puzzle like this. He tried not to notice that a small crowd had gathered around him, and he focused on the multicoloured cube. Taking a deep breath, he twisted it this way … and then that. Then this, then that, this, that, this, that, until …

"Wow!" said Mo, turning the Rubik's cube over and over. He waved it in the air so everyone could see. "Look!"

Oscar's cheeks were hot. "It's not *that* big a deal," he mumbled.

"That's true!" Harry laughed. "Hey, do you lot want to look at something *really* cool?" He hoofed the football so hard that it flew right across the playground … and over the wall.

There was a distant crash.

"That was your fault, Oscar," said Harry, stomping away.

"He'll get over it," Mo said, laughing. He spun round and spoke to the others. "Remember, if there's anything you'd like Oscar to look at, bring it to school … *He's here all week!*"

"W-w-what?" stammered Oscar.

No one heard him. They were too busy asking questions.

Chapter 5

The next day, Oscar was very, very busy indeed.
He showed Leisha how to do sudoku puzzles.

He oiled the wheels on Riley's skateboard so it
didn't squeak. He fixed everyone's scooters, too.
And one of the teacher's bikes.

When Ms Swan brought in her new laptop,
he helped her to log on to the school's Wi-Fi.
Then he showed her how to back everything up, so she
wouldn't lose anything.

"Thank you, Oscar!" the teacher said gratefully.
"You're a star."

"You're a *geek*, not a star," scoffed Harry afterwards. "And if you're so clever, tell me something funny," he added. "MAKE ME LAUGH."

Oscar thought for a moment. "I've got it," he said at last. "Why did the team spin the trophy round and round?"

"I don't know," said Harry, in a bored voice. "Why *did* the team spin the trophy round and round?"

Oscar smiled. "Because it was the Whirled Cup."

Harry snorted so loudly that Ms Swan asked him if he was quite well.

Chapter 6

"Children, I've got a wonderful surprise for you all!" said Ms Swan, on the last day of term. "Mo asked if we could have a quiz and I thought it was such a great idea, I said yes."

Everyone groaned.

"It'll be fiendishly difficult – " the teacher went on, "with a mystery prize!"

This made the whole class whoop and cheer.
One boy wriggled around so much, he fell off his seat.
Oscar could hardly breathe, he was so excited.

Ms Swan chose the teams, pointing here and there until she'd split the class into twos. "Excellent," she said, rubbing her hands together.

Harry put his hand up. "I think you've made a mistake," he said. "I'm with Oscar."

"Lucky you," said the teacher, beaming at them both. "Now, listen to the rules." She told the children that if a team answered correctly, they went through to the next round. A wrong answer and they were out.

"Harsh," said Mo, shaking his head.

At first, the quiz questions were easy.

"What's the capital of France?"

"Paris!"

But then they became trickier.

"What did Elon Musk call his first rocket?"

"Falcon 1!"

Before long, there was only one team left in the competition: Harry and Oscar.

"Answer this question to win the mystery prize," said Ms Swan. "You'll need to be a real football expert to get this right," she added solemnly.

"That's me!" said Harry, punching the air. "I know everything about football!"

"How many panels does a football have?" asked Ms Swan.

Harry opened and closed his mouth like a goldfish, but no words came out.

Oscar quietly said, "A football has 12 black pentagons and 20 white hexagons. So, the answer's 32."

There was a l-o-n-g pause, before Ms Swan boomed, "CORRECT. Congratulations, Harry and Oscar. Here's your mystery prize!"

It was a football.

Harry smiled sheepishly. "I'm sorry for making fun of you," he said to Oscar. "I wouldn't mind being like you."

This made Oscar feel happy inside. "Fancy a game of football?" he asked.

"Try to stop me," said Harry.

So they played with the prize football after school. And when it turned out that Oscar was probably the world's worst football player, Harry didn't make fun of him. He just offered to teach Oscar how to score.

"I don't know how to thank you," Oscar said to Mo on the way home for the holidays. "You made me cool!"

"I didn't," said Mo, with a grin. "How could I, when you were cool already?"

Diaries

Dear Diary

I love reading and
I love facts. But I'm worried.
Everyone at school thinks that
I'm a TOTAL GEEK. They say that
I'm too nerdy to play football
with them ... How can I change
their minds? I think I'll ask
the new boy to help. Mo is
<u>seriously cool</u>. He'll know what
to do!

Oscar

Dear Diary

Hey, I started a new school! It's going to be AWESOME, once I make some friends. There's this boy called Oscar who knows a bazillion facts! He'd be a top team member in a quiz. And he can make <u>anything</u> work. If he could be my very first friend that would be <u>seriously cool</u>.

Mo

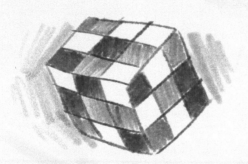

Ideas for reading

Written by Gill Matthews
Primary Literacy Consultant

Reading objectives:
- check that the text makes sense to them, discuss their understanding and explain the meaning of words in context
- ask questions to improve their understanding of a text
- draw inferences such as inferring characters' feelings, thoughts and motives from their actions, and justify inferences with evidence

Spoken language objectives:
- articulate and justify answers, arguments and opinions
- give well-structured descriptions, explanations and narratives for different purposes, including for expressing feelings
- use spoken language to develop understanding through speculating, hypothesising, imagining and exploring ideas

Curriculum links: Relationships education – Caring friendships

Interest words: fiendishly, solemnly, sheepishly

Resources: IT, Rubik's cubes

Build a context for reading

- Ask children to look at the front cover of the book. Discuss what they think Oscar might be like.
- Read the back-cover blurb and ask children to suggest why they think Oscar might not feel as though he fits in.
- Ask how they think the new boy might help Oscar to show who he really is.
- Draw attention to the fact that this is a contemporary story. Discuss what features the story might have.

Understand and apply reading strategies

- Read pp2–7 aloud, using appropriate expression. Ask what the children to describe Oscar and compare this with their initial suggestions.
- How do the children think Oscar feels at home and at school? Encourage children to justify their responses by giving reasons and evidence from the text.